Don't Panic, Annika!

D1099804

For my very own Annika (who never panics) J.C.B.

For Tyler Motohiro J.M.

Don't Panic, Annika!

Juliet Clare Bell

Illustrated by Jennifer E. Morris

PICCADILLY PRESS • LONDON

Annika was
a panicker.
She *always*
panicked . . .

When she dropped Moose in the pond . . . she panicked.

"He's fallen in! I can't get him!" she shouted.

"Try fishing him out with your net," said Dad.

"I CAN'T!" shouted Annika.

"DON'T PANIC, ANNIKA," said Dad. "Take a nice deep breath."

So Annika took a deep breath.
(And another one, just to be sure.)
Then she fished Moose out
of the pond.

"Brilliant!" said Dad.

When she couldn't do up
her coat . . . she panicked.
"The zip's stuck! We'll miss
the party!" she shouted.
"Try again,"
said her brother.

"I CAN'T!" shouted Annika.

"DON'T PANIC, ANNIKA," said her brother.

"Count to ten, really slowly."

So Annika counted to ten, really slowly.

Then she passed Moose to her brother and

zipped up her coat in one go.

"Brilliant!" said her brother.

When she couldn't find Moose at bedtime . . .

she panicked.

"He should be in bed!
He's gone!" she shouted.
"Try to remember where you
left him," said Mum.
"I CAN'T!" shouted Annika.
"He's disappeared!"

"DON'T PANIC, ANNIKA," said Mum.

"Close your eyes and think how good
it will be when you've found him."

So Annika closed her eyes and thought about
falling asleep snuggled up with Moose.

Then she remembered.

"I know! He's brushing his teeth!"

"Brilliant!" said Mum.

One windy day, Annika and her mum
and brother set off to fly their kites.

"Wait! I forgot Moose!"
shouted Annika,
and she ran back into the
house to fetch him.

"Quick!" said Mum,
"or we'll miss the bus!"

Annika grabbed Moose,
but the wind blew
and the door
SLAMMED . . .

SHUT!

Annika opened her mouth but no words came out.

She clutched Moose's paw tightly.

"Don't worry, Moose," she whispered.

"Mum will open the door."

"Oh no!" shouted her mum from outside.
"The keys are in my orange bag!
They're in the house!"

Annika looked up and saw the bag.
"I'M STUCK! I'll never get out!
They'll never get in!"
shouted Annika,
and then she
started to . . .

. . . think.

She held Moose
even tighter.
Then she took a deep breath.
(And another one,
just to be sure.)

"Don't worry, Moose,"
she said. "I'll get the
bag down."

But the bag
was too high.

Annika nearly
panicked, but
instead, she . . .

1 2 3 4 5 6 7 8 9 10

counted
to
ten,
really
slowly.

And she remembered.
There were spare keys
in the kitchen!
But they were high up as well.

Annika nearly
panicked,
but instead,
she . . .

. . . closed her eyes and thought about flying kites
with her mum and brother.

Then she stretched up
and hooked the keys
into her fishing net.

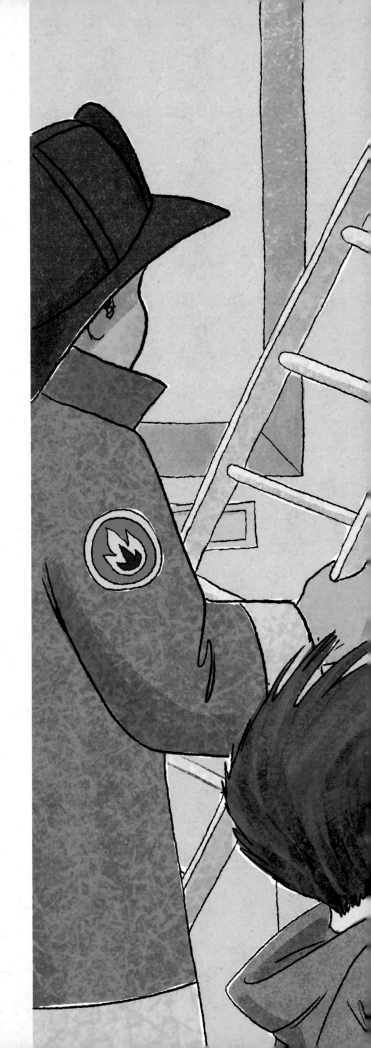

"BRILLIANT!"
said Annika.

Back in the hall,
Annika heard a *terrible* racket
coming from outside.

"DON'T PANIC, ANNIKA!" shouted everyone.

"I'm not panicking," said Annika.

"BUT YOU CAN'T GET OUT AND WE CAN'T GET IN!"

shouted her mum.

"STOP!"

shouted
Annika.

"DON'T PANIC," said Annika.
"Take a nice deep breath."
So they did.
(And another one, just to be sure.)

"Then count to ten, really slowly," said Annika.

So they did.

"Now, close your eyes and think how good it will be

when we're together again," said Annika.

So they did.

"And now,"
called Annika,
"open the letterbox. . .

and take *these*!"
Annika stood back . . .

. . . and the door opened. "Brilliant!" said everyone.

Annika **was** a panicker.

. . . but not any more.

First published in Great Britain in 2011
This edition published 2015
Deepdene Lodge, Deepdene Avenue,
Dorking, Surrey, RH5 4AT, UK
www.bonnierpublishing.com

Text © Juliet Clare Bell, 2011
Illustrations © Jennifer Morris, 2011

All rights reserved. No part of this publication may be reproduced,
stored in a retrieval system, or transmitted, in any form or by any
means, electronic, mechanical, photocopying or otherwise, without
prior permission of the copyright owner.

The right of Juliet Clare Bell to be recognised as Author and
Jennifer E. Morris as the Illustrator of this work has been asserted
by them in accordance with the Copyright, Designs and Patents Act 1988.

Printed and bound in China

ISBN: 978 1 84812 497 4 (paperback)

1 3 5 7 9 10 8 6 4 2